KAY THOMPSON'S ELOISE

Eloise at the Wedding

STORY BY **Margaret McNamara**

ILLUSTRATED BY **Tammie Lyon**

Aladdin Paperbacks

NEW YORK · LONDON · TORONTO · SYDNEY

For the dress

ALADDIN PAPERBACKS
An imprint of Simon & Schuster Children's Publishing Division
1230 Avenue of the Americas, New York, NY 10020
The text of this book was set in Century Old Style.
Manufactured in the United States of America
First Aladdin Paperbacks edition June 2006
12 14 16 18 20 19 17 15 13 11
Library of Congress Cataloging-in-Publication Data
McNamara, Margaret.
Eloise at the wedding / written by Margaret McNamara ;
illustrated by Tammie Lyon.—1st Aladdin Paperbacks ed.
p. cm.—(Kay Thompson's Eloise) (Ready-to-read)
Summary: Although she hasn't been invited to the wedding being held in the Plaza
Hotel where she lives, Eloise finds a way to play an important role in the ceremony.
ISBN-13: 978-0-689-87449-9 (pbk.)
ISBN-10: 0-689-87449-9 (pbk.)
ISBN-13: 978-1-4169-2457-9 (library)
ISBN-10: 1-4169-2457-4 (library)
0513 LAK
[1. Weddings—Fiction. 2. Plaza Hotel (New York, N.Y.)—Fiction.
3. Hotels, motels, etc.—Fiction. 4. New York (N.Y.)—Fiction. 5. Humorous stories.]
I. Lyon, Tammie, ill. II. Title. III. Series. IV. Series: Ready-to-read.
PZ7.M47879343Ej 2005
[E]—dc22
2004016673

I am Eloise.
I live at The Plaza Hotel.

The Grand Ballroom
is busy today.

Cleaners are cleaning.

Cooks are cooking.

Waiters are waiting
for something to happen.

"What is going on?" I say.
"There will be
a wedding today,"
Nanny says.

"I am going," I say.
I love, love, love weddings.

"You are not going,"
Nanny says.
"No one has asked you
to go."

That is true.
No one has asked me.

Not yet.

"It is time for your bath,"
Nanny says.

In the bath I am:
a sea captain,

a mermaid,

the Statue of Liberty.

After the bath
I am clean, clean, clean.

Nanny says,
"If you are very good
you may see the bride."

I am as good as I can be.

We peek inside
the Grand Ballroom.
There are men
who look like penguins.

There are ladies
with large hats.

There is a groom.
There is no bride.

Nanny says, "Oh dear, oh dear, oh dear."

I hear a noise.
It is a sad noise.
It is a crying noise.

It is coming from
the powder room.
I look inside.

There is the bride.
She is crying.

"Oh dear, oh dear,
   oh dear," she says.
"What is wrong?" I say.

"The flower girl is sick,"
she says.
"How can I get married?"

"Do you want me to be
your flower girl?" I say.
"I do!" the bride says.

I am rather good
at being a flower girl.

Oooooooo I love,
love, love weddings.